SHITSTORM

A novelette

FERNANDO SDRIGOTTI

First Published in 2018
by Open Pen, 25 Crescent Road, London, E13 0LU
openpen.co.uk
978-1-9164136-1-0
OPNOV002

OPEN PEN NOVELETTES #1

"Shitstorm"
First Edition

Cover illustration by Pierre Buttin - pierrebuttin.com

Y después se desata la tormenta de mierda.

Roberto Bolaño, *Nocturno de Chile*

A dentist from Minneapolis books a hunting safari in Zimbabwe.

His name is Walter Turner, a wealthy nobody, completely unknown beyond the confines of his practice and neighbourhood in the suburbs — one more god-fearing American with a dazzling smile and a big cardboard-looking house. Perhaps he read too much Ernest Hemingway as a teenager or perhaps he watched too many films about men performing heroic feats in hot places. Or perhaps he's trying to work through some issues. Or maybe hunting provides him with an escape from his life. Or maybe a combination all of these things, and some other things, and having lots of spare cash, and being bored of his family — his peroxide blonde second wife and his healthy-looking all-American adolescent children, twins Pam and Gerard, who will next year attend Berkeley to study Medicine and Law respectively. For whatever the reason he books the safari and off he goes to the Dark Continent to do his killing that some like to call a sport, like many American men with dazzling smiles have done before, some even achieving some minor form of glory in the process.

The dentist, our dentist, has a passion for trophy hunting and his speciality is the bow and arrow. He has hunted right, left and centre, all over the world, mostly in the Global South, where there's plenty of animals to kill, where you can always hire one or two lackeys to carry your things around in the heat, as has been done by white hunters for centuries, and when no one questions the sense of anyone with money. Yes, hunting with a bow and arrow instead of a proper gun is incredibly stupid but money can make it look less stupid, because it can buy a nice bow and arrow. And Dr Turner has experience – he knows the drill, is in control of the situation, speaks the lingo, fits the bill of the white hunter very well, which means he wears a lot of beige and looks good in pictures, especially when he grows his beard for a week or two. Yet even if experienced and photogenic the dentist has never hunted a lion before, and for this trophy – for a male wild lion – he's willing to pay US$ 55,000, which is a lot of money, even for a rich man like him. Lots of money, but a lion and the dopamine kick he'll get from killing one are worth it. So off he goes to Zimbabwe and soon he's in the middle of the jungle, swatting flies in the heat, stoically coping with a case of heartburn due to a lack of fibre in his diet.

The local guides and the crew and the professional

hunter he has hired prove to be at the top of their game. Taciturn and efficient, they don't waste time going for smaller prey; the only thing they have time for is a male lion, the bigger the better – this is a business that works through word of mouth and they really want to finish this job, get to the next one, and so on, hopefully one day stop babysitting Americans. And soon they're right on track: lions don't abound anywhere in the world but you are more certain to bump into one in Zimbabwe than in the State of Minnesota. Now it's just a game of waiting.

And waiting, a couple of days into their adventure, early in the morning, either one of the local guides or the professional hunter spots footprints in the mud by a puddle of water. The prints are big enough to confirm that the lion is a male, but the footprints soon disappear into Hwange National Park, a protected area that isn't covered by their permit. When the hunting party clock that the lion is in the park a decision must be made: go back on their tracks to try to find another male lion old enough to be hunted legally; or to continue tracking this one, to entice him out of the park, taking a considerable risk but saving a lot of time in the process. It's only a matter of getting him out and killing him, after all; as long as they don't get caught bribing him out of the park they'll be alright. Maybe the dentist participates in the decision or maybe he's never told. Somehow the lion gets baited out of the park and is shot with an arrow while he's eating from an ox carcass.

The arrow doesn't really do its work, much to the dismay of the guides and the professional hunter, and perhaps even Dr Turner. Maybe he wasn't that good a shot or maybe the lion was stronger than usual or maybe it was all down to bad luck – who knows? The point is that the arrow doesn't kill the lion and the hunting party end up tracking the wounded beast, searching for traces of blood, praying that he won't go back into the park alive, with an arrow tagged with the dentist's name hanging from the side.

A day and a half goes by, the party start to despair and Dr Turner starts to consider the possible consequences of his infantile fixation with toy weapons. That is until, finally, they locate and kill the lion. With a gunshot to the heart, the professional hunter once more establishes powder's supremacy over primitive weaponry. And so they set out to skin and behead the beast, as it is customary among hunters, the whole reason of hunting being not really to kill the animal but to boast among acquaintances, turning once living matter into a decoration, a *trophy*. And here they discover the lion wears a collar, a little piece of rubber that just about manages to circle around its neck, almost invisible underneath the mane.

Yes, the lion is a collared specimen, which means he's a protected beast, not just a nicely accessorised one. He goes by the name of Cyril and is loved by Danny Gervais, Maria Farrow, Shane Osbourne and other animal-loving celebs who have been involved in some charitable initiative with animals all around the world, as will be discovered soon. Cyril is even an academic lion, being the focus of a study in Oxford, for some obscure reason. Even before finding out all this, just with the collar, Dr Turner panics and gives orders to hide the corpse, and he quickly leaves Zimbabwe, not before shooting a couple of selfies with the lion, to prove he has *taken* him.

Cyril's absence goes quickly noticed by the park authorities and a search party is arranged. The remains are found a week later, half unburied by other animals busy enacting the cycle of life. A natural death is ruled out and the hunt for the hunter begins.

The park guards suspect local poachers, suppliers to a wide array of industries, not all of them illegal or located in the former Colonies, or below the Equator line. The Zimbabwean press, on the other hand, blame a Chinese hunter who just happened to be round the area. Others blame others, conforming their prejudices in who they blame. It looks as if no culprit will ever be found and the news won't make it out of Zimbabwe, as is usually the case. But a journalist from National Geographic, coincidentally in the area for an orientalist documentary, picks up the scoop and the killing achieves international status quite quickly. Danny Gervais, Maria Farrow and Shane Osbourne find out about the murder of their exotic pet and tweet about it and their outrage and their sadness and their pain and their their their their.

And like this another shitstorm is born.

o o o

A shitstorm.

At first it takes the form of an outrage without a clear target, purely because there isn't one. And for that reason the outrage is directed against all hunters. Petitions to ban hunting are started, signed and shared and forgotten in the space of hours, but not failing to leave the signatories with a taste of justice and satisfaction in their mouths. Images of men and women of dubious intelligence but with expensive guns start circulating the timelines and newsfeeds as possible culprits. And while the blame game is being played, and the news travels the world from one corner to the other, the Daily Mail — tipped off by a friend of Dr Turner who received an incriminating photo over WhatsApp — puts an end to the mystery and the shitstorm finds its name. And soon Dr Turner's name starts trending and with the status of now being a trending topic comes the attention and with the attention the dangers.

The images of the dead lion and the dentist posing all smiles next to it, let's say, help fan the fire. As does the fact that Dr Turner — pure white American fake teeth, nicely tanned, expensive watch on his left wrist, balding and unapologetic and gun-loving and Republican — might exude money through every pore but has as much charisma as a catalogue of nails. So now the prey is the dentist who read too much Hemingway or watched too many films about men doing heroic things in the heat or has *issues* or hates his family or is bored of life or all of the above. And now the hunters are the mob, as we are every now and then called by those who disagree with our ideas. We The Mob, frothing at the mouth with rage, braying, hoping that he gets caught and that he pays for his arrogance and cruelty, and that he pays dearly. The mob thirsty for justice, or for revenge, or for something to do, a distraction, a raison d'etre.

Sooner or later, death threats ensue, for him and for his family. For his daughter and his wife even rape threats, much to the dismay of some other members of the mob who would never go that far. And speaking of death threats even PETA joins in this contemporary tradition, claiming that he needs to be extradited, judged by environmentalists, and preferably hanged with quorn rope or fed alive to wild pigs or feral dogs or turned into compost. Some find PETA's post extreme but many also agree with their assessment and would happily be there at the gallows to tighten the noose and perhaps even kick the stool. Others don't know what or who PETA is but take positions around their comments nevertheless, and some even figure out what PETA are on about in the process of commenting, which means that in the end the death threats are a good PR exercise.

For Dr Walter it's now too late to realise that you might kill as many animals as you want, as long as you don't kill a celebrity's favourite pet. Or as long as you don't find yourself in the wrong place, at the wrong time, because timing is everything, and timing was everything in his case too. Things had been slow when the Daily Mail article started to make the rounds on social media. There hadn't been anything for us to outrage about for a couple of days. The President of the United States of America had been quiet, perhaps golfing or gorging on burgers and Diet Coke. Or maybe it's his name that did it: easy to remember, easy to repeat, short enough to type and practical when it comes to Twitter's limited character count and our short attention span. Or maybe it was the photo. The way he looks in the photo, his smug smile, his clothes or the fact he used a selfie stick. Or maybe it was about the arrogance of knowing you've fucked up and still keeping a register: [smile] here I'm posing with a lion I killed illegally – I shouldn't be doing this, I really shouldn't but I'm doing it anyway because I can [shutter pressed, a moment of life and death fixed for posterity]. And then, to add to the stupidity, sending the photo to someone with a grudge or who doesn't have a grudge but needs cash and the photo.

So maybe it was about his stupidity, maybe it always boils down to people doing stupid things, being incredibly stupid all the time, or just once, being stupid at the wrong moment. And our never-ending hunger for content.

And now the price to pay is unwanted recognition, being kicked into the spotlight, in the open, in the middle of a shitstorm and without an umbrella.

o o o

A shitstorm.

It goes on for days and days on end. The outrage grows and spills beyond Twitter. Dr Turner's practice is boycotted.

Bad reviews are left on his Yelp profile. He gets kicked out of the local Rotary Club. And then he's forced to leave the house with his family when they receive a threatening toy lion stuffed with white powder in the post – the Turners end up under police protection, even if the powder was just gluten-free flour and not Anthrax. But the police can't brush it aside, because the case has captured the attention of the country and the world.

Fox News covers his case, focusing on the death and rape threats and how these attacks speak of the violent ideas of all American liberals and leftists, those morally corrupted atheists intent on destroying everything that makes this nation great. And then the President of the United States of America – who is known for getting his daily briefings from Fox News – tweets his support for Dr Turner, appalled at those who put animal welfare before the welfare of people – at least this can be gathered from his tweets. But haven't similar pictures of the President of the United States of America's older sons posing with a dead elephant been seen before? So more than being of any help the President of the United States of America's intervention just fans the fire a bit more, and the shitstorm gets more momentum and it looks as if it could engulf the whole world.

And while our attention is focused on Dr Turner many more lions get killed in Africa, shot mostly by wealthy men like our dentist. Killed dead by these men who all dress the same, or by those working for them. Lions as lionesque as Cyril. Lions who smelled as bad as Cyril. Lions who hunted and killed and fucked and slept and shat like Cyril. Lions with manes; others without manes. Lions deserving our outrage and our time. And yet no one finds out, because it's impossible to keep up with everything. So it's Dr Turner alone now, a stand in for every imbecile on earth with a gun and time and money to go shoot it in some hot and humid spot of the earth, where mosquitoes are brutal and where water can kill you.

o o o

Soon the case of the white hunter with his bow and arrow and his issues or ennui or a combination of several things finds its way to the UK, the Shangri La of the opinion piece, where every once well-reputed newspaper or sensationalistic rag is now a blog kept by unpaid interns, where every half-chewed thought has a home as long as it is a cheaply-acquired whim likely to get clicks. In the UK the news arrives and soon the opinion bots start churning out articles about the hunter, vivisecting the facts and the events, attempting to read several centuries of violent history (mostly American and British) through the case of one until then irrelevant Minnesotan arsehole.

Most progressive opinion pieces could be synthesised into one: Walter Turner is a stand-in for the patriarchy and white privilege, but this doesn't grant the death threats to his family and himself, *we* – a collective assemblage of unclear form – need to do better. Most rightwing opinion pieces – that is, the vast majority – could be summed into the attempt to diminish the fact that Dr Turner was in the wrong when shooting a protected lion, that a penchant for hunting is more or less synonym for being a cunt, focusing instead on a potential blunder by his coloured hunting partners, and paying special attention to the way in which some animal-loving psychopaths have declared war on him. It's always the same, or almost the same, because there's always room for a different hot-take, particularly when the opinion piece is written by any of the sport's top athletes. There's always the top athletes.

Brandon O'Neill raises the bet with a piece in defence of hunting, saying a bullet to the head is the greatest honour for a wild animal; something about treating the animal like an animal; something about hunting being a game of love between the hunter and its target; something about honour; something about how criticisms of hunting per se are actually middle class moral panics. This spawns a mini-shitstorm of its own, with the bien pensant among us quickly demanding he loses his columns with The Spectator and The Daily Mail, that his latest book gets boycotted by Amazon, turned into pulp, that he's disinvited by this or that minor rightwing think tank, from some dodgy conference where he's supposed to deliver a lecture titled "My Duty to Be Unpleasant", not that anyone knew about the conference before we loudly told the world about it.

Nothing of this happens. O'Neill isn't disinvited from wherever we think he should be, nor is his book turned into pulp, even if no one really read it. But Owen James bites O'Neill's hook and responds with something arguing the opposite, referring to O'Neill's infantile contrarian drivel. And then someone else — someone not as good as James — writes something else, from another angle, and so on, many responses to O'Neill, all full of venom and words, lots of words, grouped in chunks of nine to one thousand. As a result O'Neil's article gets a lot of traction and his editors are very happy and they commission a new piece, deadline by the end of the week.

Back across the Atlantic Dr Turner is screwed, he's over, done, his career in tatters, every piece that is published

— all over the world — feels like a kick to the chin, and he'll probably end up topping his head with one of his own guns or his fucking bow and arrow, all because of his unbearable arrogance and stupidity. But then the bombs go off in the Eurostar terminal at St Pancras International and the President of the United States of America — two or three minutes later, due to the time difference and his television-watching habits — says that London is now a no go area, that Londoners now live in fear of fundamentalists, cowed, that immigration and London's Muslim Mayor are to blame for this attack and every attack before.

You can't imagine the shitstorm these words cause, and because no one can focus on too many shitstorms at the same time, and we're all still getting out of some of the recent ones having to do with a racist cream ad where a black woman turned white after using the product, a body-shamming outdoors ad by a protein shake company from Saudi Arabia, a pornstar who might have said something homophobic and was bullied until she committed suicide live on Periscope — because of all of these recent shitstorms, and because even with a never-ending supply of opinion pieces and hot takes and editorials there's only room for one proper shitstorm at a time, because of all this, Dr Turner starts to be forgotten. Saved by the bell or by the lack of a bell. And no one will ever remember him any more in just a matter of days. No one will give a toss anymore, very soon, even if the Daily Mail will publish an article about him shopping on a Sunday, some years from now. A typical filler written by an underpaid human content algorithm, about how careless he looks, just shopping around in his sports car, without giving a thought for Cyril or all the unnamed animals he's killed, on a Sunday afternoon, downtown with his third wife, also a peroxide blonde, but this one twenty years younger than him and with bigger tits.

When this article is published some will have a tiny involuntary memory – their insignificant Proustian moment – but no one will pay much attention, and no one will read beyond the first two or three paragraphs. The article will gather only fifteen or sixteen comments by the usual hardcore of fiends who linger below the line, and soon it will be relegated to the bottom of the Daily Mail's homepage, a fact that due to the sorry design of the interface will grant its disappearance from the public eye.

And then nothing, almost as if Dr Turner had never existed.

o o o

Fifteen dead and sixty-five wounded.

The bomb went off in a packed carriage towards the front, in order to maximise the damage thanks to the inertia, according to a reporter who presents this hypothesis with enough conviction for it to catch on and be repeated by other less self-assured reporters. The bomb might have gone off earlier than expected, he adds, and this might have saved lives. Beyond this primordial speculation all the rest is (also) speculation.

The corpses are still warm when Brandon O'Neill uploads a lengthy Facebook post about this latest attack on Western Civilisation. This shouldn't make us stop doing the things we love; Islamists hate our way of life and our fear is their gain; liberals and leftists should direct their outrage not against the President of the United States of America and his provocative words, but against the monsters – yes, these are monsters we are talking about, no need to see them in human terms, no humanity can explain their monstrosity – who actually carried out this deed, who live among us, and who want to see us dead, even if we welcomed them, opened our doors to them, respected them, treated them as equals, gave them a safe haven, a way out of their war-torn countries. Liberals and leftists have no answers, O'Neill goes on, and if they had them the answers would show their ideas as the incoherent ramblings they are, ergo their silence. And so on and on and on. The post is over 3,000 words long and he could have copy-pasted it from the thing he wrote after the Charlie Hebdo attacks, or the thing he wrote after Bataclan, or Manchester, or London Bridge. But nobody will realise this, because his words ring true to those who want them to ring true, and we all tend to forget words after a while. Words become background noise to these terrible events, that in due time we'll forget as well.

In ten minutes the post is liked by three hundred and forty-three Facebook users and it's shared by seventy-two. There seems to be a consensus in the comments section that O'Neill always has the angle that is likely to trigger liberals and leftists and champagne socialists and the politically correct and snowflakes and and and and, because he's always asking the uncomfortable questions etc etc etc. There are a couple of negative comments, the unconverted to the Church of O'Neill, who bitterly point out how he always manipulates events to fit his agenda, how he always uses the same two or three argumentative lines to lay a few blows on the left, the same kind of people who routinely ask why he never seems to hound fascists (or what they consider to be fascists) in the same way. But these comments are negligible and soon vanish, deleted into oblivion, very likely by O'Neill himself.

And then, just to confirm to his faithful that their idol was right, Owen James pens a Twitter thread in which he begs the People of Great Britain not to take matters into our own hands, announcing his solidarity with anyone likely to suffer after this attack. We shouldn't fall for the trap of letting the few become a stand-in for the many, we need to keep our communities together. Britain is a nation renowned for its tolerance – he doesn't mention British colonialism and imperialism this time, although he has mentioned them before, on occasions that perhaps merited the mention less. But it's a nice thread, even if it extends for over thirty seven tweets. Some find James's words brave in their call for restraint. Others accuse him of being a hypocrite who cares about everyone but the actual victims, something on which he has built a career that involves not only churning out constantly shifting opinion to a deadline but also giving talks and lectures for well-wishing middle-class lefties. A minor shitstorm ensues around James's twitter thread. He replies to some of the comments but then ends up disabling his account, as he does at least twice a month, when people bully him too much by publicly disagreeing with him.

You could say that factions start to form around these apparently opposing sides, declaring our allegiance to the usual ideas, and proscribing the usual analyses and solutions. And soon enough the death threats to both O'Neill and James roll in. Death threats generally from users without a profile picture, and who would probably issue death threats to their parents if their parents were on Twitter, just for the sake of it. Many of these eggs get quickly taken down by Twitter Support, accused of being Russian bots when in reality they're just idiots living in cellars. Some celebrate their disappearance while others — particularly among the libertarian right — bemoan it as an act of censorship. Until at 10am, with the security services still clearing the area, and with all of us either sending prayers and thoughts, or saying that prayers and thoughts aren't what is needed, while we're accommodating around the atrocity in whichever way we find fitting, out of nowhere: an organisation under the name of Breivik Brigades claims authorship of the attack through a Twitter account with twenty-two followers that very soon gets suspended too. But not before their

Pastebin communiqué is copied and shared away.

As expected it's a rather deranged text but on this occasion suspiciously well written and punctuated, with no visible grammatical errors and not much abuse of uppercase. The communiqué claims that the deed was undertaken to bring attention to White Genocide and the decimation of the British indigenous population through uncontrolled immigration and Cultural Marxism. It doesn't explain how this might be happening but it's clear as to why the Eurostar was targeted: because it's an icon of the Metropolitan Elite and their fetish for European cheese and miscegenation (it uses the word miscegenation). It also claims that Bankers and the Mainstream Media are now in control of the government, that they are the Master Puppeteers (uppercase in original). And it ends with a call to arms, God is on our side, Victory is already ours.

Needless to say, this development takes everyone by surprise, even if some of the motifs have been favourites of both right and left for many years.

Yet in a matter of minutes the BBC scrambles a panel of experts. Mid morning and several professors, dressed in hues of beige, discuss the inevitability of right wing extremism turning violent. Is this a development you were expecting? asks the presenter. This isn't, really, a *new* development but a return to old and not so old *modi operandi*, answers Professor John Derbyshire, from LSE, reminding the audience about the Bologna bombing, back in 1980, however different the recent attack might be, in magnitude and intention. Professor Jeremy Simpson from Royal Holloway doesn't agree, suggesting that the Italian authorities never really got to the bottom of the Bologna attack, that it could very well have been the Red Brigades or some of the other extreme left wing organisations operating in Italy at the time, that it's rather preposterous to try to connect these two events — separated almost by 40 years!—, when the situation here is much murkier than everyone would like to accept. Professor Derbyshire insists with his line of reasoning, saying that nevertheless there are antecedents of political violence from the right, just look at the name of this organisation, if not! The attacks in Norway were the product of a deluded individual — he acted alone, replies Professor Simpson. He had a very long and rather articulate manifesto — not that different in tone from the communiqué we've just heard, especially in its paranoia — which indicates that he was anything but hopelessly deluded and that he acted alone does not rule out his was a clearly political act, and an act of terrorism, replies Professor Derbyshire. And a polite argument between the scholars ensues, a televised version of their frequent discussions in conferences attended by ten or twenty scholars, in which occasionally both end up in the same panel. Meanwhile the presenter moves his head up and down and to the sides to show that he understands the complexity of what's being discussed, although he doesn't. But the director seems to love the nodding, as we all do, and between shots of the scholars we get a lot of the presenter's face, his grave expression, his pristine hair, which makes good live television.

And suddenly more developments.

At 10:53, while the academics are still busy agreeing, ISIS also claims responsibility for the attack. The presenter interrupts a Professor Stanley, from University of Westminster, to inform the audience of this new twist, as they cut to the usual video shot with a potato, where a guy with dusty army boots, wearing a balaclava, and brandishing a rusty AK47 that he probably can't shoot very well, rants about something in a language he very likely speaks with an European accent. The subtitles translate for the audience the usual platitudes and received stupidities disguised as threats and radical ideas. The usual words are read and heard. The usual commonplaces are arrived at. And then the blurry video cuts to the usual epic music and images of

IEDs and martyrs and snipers, and things blowing up in the air, and other things that are golden and others silvery, until the image disappears abruptly and the BBC presenter is left staring in panic towards the back of the studio. He stares somewhere past the camera, waiting for the producer to feed him a wrapper, but this doesn't happen. So he finally gathers the mental energy to improvise and ask the panellists what they think about this sudden development. There seems to be certain agreement among the former private now momentarily public intellectuals gathered for the occasion, that this is a very interesting development – they all nod in agreement, yes, it's a very interesting development. And the presenter nods too, yes, very interesting, very unexpected, very – he nods. There is some silent nodding among everyone on the studio, and too much nodding going on, for too long, there can be such a thing as too much nodding, so they get taken off the air by the shrewd director concerned about ratings, to give way to a live transmission from St Pancras International, and everybody is happy now, everybody in the set can relax and stop playing their parts. It's already 11:07am and the police are still working and the emergency services are still picking up pieces of flesh, bones, and bloodied items of clothing, and putting them in bags. We can't see them picking up pieces of flesh, bones and items of clothing and putting them in bags but we can imagine it, because the reporter on the site – with her immaculate hair and a perfect fake tan matching her accent – details this for us.

By now Brandon O'Neill has already managed to write a lengthy editorial for The Contrarian, the magazine he founded and runs with the help of corporate funds that include oil and tobacco companies, not that there's anything wrong with this because he's a libertarian. In this new intervention, he claims that regardless who is behind the attacks, it's actually ISIS who are the true enemies of Enlightenment; that if right wingers have taken to blowing up things – if we are to believe the reports – it's because they aren't allowed to express certain views any more, chastised as they are by the liberal elites, accused of being nazis or even worse things, just because they voted to get their country out of the European Union in the hope of getting rid of all immigration (but it was actually about independence, somehow).

By this time too, perhaps a few minutes later, Owen James writes a piece for the Guardian where he argues that these Breivik Brigades are the logical conclusion of years of politicians' pandering to racists and xenophobes, demagogues who have moved the Overton Window so much towards the right that people might end up falling in the English Channel, a metaphor that is hard to justify and makes little sense but that the editors must have waved through because it's Owen James after all and they really needed copy and James doesn't take editing lightly.

Some agree with O'Neill, others agree with James; we do our nodding, and soon it's 3 o'clock in the afternoon.

Some of us have changed our avatars to one with the Union Jack or a photo of Big Ben while others have chosen a black square while others did nothing. Many of us have announced ourselves safe over Facebook while others have articulated in the strongest of terms that we are against doing this, in order not to play at the hands of the terrorists, whoever these might be. And of course all of us are now policing people's reactions to an atrocity, as is the tradition these days. Why do we care so much about London when last week bombs went off in x or y? ask some of us. Why don't people care about London when they cared about the bombs that went off last week in x or y? ask others. Why do we only care about terrorist attacks when they happen at our doorstep? Why do we care about all terrorist attacks except for those that happen here?

o o o

Perhaps not a panic but the tension is palpable. The fear — even if repressed — exists, and the possibility of being blown up to smithereens is something we consider to be pretty realistic when leaving our houses, even if to the outside it's all stay calm and carry on and keep on living.

The attack and the possibility of more bombs become the favourite conversation topic of radio and TV shows, podcasts, vlogs, speculative Youtube videos, conspiracy theory blogs, chit-chat at the supermarket queue, the interrogations of migration officers, and social media (they stop trending after a week or so, but they are still there, lurking in the background). It gives us something to talk about, a reason to keep marvelling at the evil of other human beings. Perhaps we start waiting for another bomb, a larger one. Perhaps we start desiring that another bomb goes off, not really because we want someone to die or get terribly maimed by a wanton explosion in the middle of the day but because we want something to happen, we want more chances to be proven right, to argue this or argue that, to prove points — it's always about proving points. Or perhaps we just want the unavoidable to happen quickly — we want to hasten the end. Bombs, then, might be a form of collective euthanasia. Maybe we are desperate and can't wait to die. And maybe all this explains the tension, an atmospheric pressure alike to those days before a summer storm. The air feels loaded. It becomes difficult to breathe. The pressure on the chest is unbearable. We are waiting for something to happen.

Meanwhile a mosque in Birmingham gets petrol bombed on Wednesday and on Thursday someone tries to run over a group of girls leaving a Muslim youth centre in Milton Keynes; instead of hitting the girls he ends up crashing against a phone box – no one gets hurt, not even the driver, who manages to run away and disappear into the city centre. On Twitter, Owen James writes of this attack as proof that he wasn't wrong, that it was going to happen, that sooner or later someone was going to end up taking matters into their own hands, and that is the reason we must cool things down, pretend nothing's going on. He will go on to write an opinion piece about this too.

Brandon O'Neill instead writes a chronicle for The Contrarian, about a couple on their honeymoon who died in the St Pancras's blast. They were from Margate, born and bred, were under 25, and their tragic trip was supposed to be their first time abroad. Thomas, the groom, was an electrician and Carly, the bride, worked for the local council. Their families had put the money together for them to travel to Paris, of all places, to celebrate their union. The story – which features images of the floral arrangements left by family and friends for the dead couple – is a very moving piece of writing in which O'Neill shows his sensitive side while he wonders why the *progressive* press (italics in the original) can forget so quickly about victims, why they rather focus on potential acts of revenge that never happen, why they mistrust people so much unless they truly mistrust humanity, why they didn't pay attention to this working class pair, dead on the happiest day of their lives? He never mentions the attacks against the mosque or the Muslim girls. But you can't fit everything in a nine hundred word piece.

And then on Friday a blogger from Archway goes viral after the news circulates that she's been making bread from vaginal yeast, selling it on her site – now we can all stop thinking about bombs for a while.

The product is called CUNTDOUGH and apparently not a few have found the idea worthy of their money – CUNTDOUGH becomes an internet sensation after The Guardian runs a story on it. But in a matter of hours she gets in trouble with the Foods Standards Agency for trading without a permit and potentially breaking health and safety protocol, by producing bread out of something that comes from her own body, from her cunt, to be precise.

The blogger claims hers is a performance and that the bread wasn't really intended for eating – it's art. But one of the buyers, one of the CUNTDOUGH pioneers, claims to have eaten it, thinking CUNTDOUGH was just a hip name like any other, a very common phenomenon these days; so the CUNTDOUGH pioneer threatens to sue the now self-proclaimed performance artist. Jonathon Jones, the renowned art critic who hates art, seizes the occasion and writes a piece for The Guardian claiming that as contemporary art is crap it was only a matter of time until someone made art from her cunt and we shouldn't be surprised if someone actually made art from their arsehole. His hot take back dates several decades, and ignores the work of several artists with cunts between their legs (and arses too), from the ones who have painted with menstrual blood to those who have shat in tins, some currently exhibited in Tate Modern. But Jones's article doesn't get much traction or causes a shitstorm because it's published at 2am in the morning, as has been the custom in the past year since he irked a large part of the Guardian readership with some opinion or other.

The next morning a group of liberal feminists from Highgate and Hampstead Heath come to the former-blogger-now-performance artist's support, arguing that her persecution is one motivated by patriarchal misconceptions and prejudices, that banning CUNTDOUGH is an infringement of free speech, one more stain in a long history of persecuting women. Some agree with the feminists; others ask if they would say the same if someone had made bread from cock cheese. Marion Berry points out that making bread from cock cheese is impossible while Judith Burchill writes a piece for the Independent where she defends the blogger and what she deems her unapologetic celebration of biological femininity. Obviously she writes the article to troll trans women and their allies, as she generally does in most of what she writes, eliciting the ire of some of the liberal feminists from Highgate and Hampstead but not all of them, as this is a topic on which the sorority is divided. And then, later, around two or three pm, someone called Voosh – renowned in MRA circles for his pick up books – writes a piece for his very popular blog called The Return of the Alpha Male, where he presents the amateur baker as a paradigm of everything that's wrong both with feminism and women in western society today. In the article, in which he links back mostly to half-literate things he has written for his blog, he goes on to propose a return to traditional and patriarchal ways of life, hand-in-hand with the regressive social policies of the President of the United States of America. Housework sets you free, he ends the piece ironically, although few of his followers get the nod towards Auschwitz, not that they would object in any way if they did. This rather obvious missed reference doesn't stop his army of involuntary celibate minions from rape-threat-bombing some vocal women on Twitter. Others suffer pangs of outrage about the post but help share it, not failing to express our outrage while doing so. David Baron, the famous nazi, doesn't miss the reference and apart from agreeing with Voosh's proposal for a return to a patriarchal society makes use of the occasion to claim that the figures of the Holocaust are greatly inflated. And while we are all distracted discussing cunt bakery, the final solution, and Judith Burchill's article and her transphobia, Scotland Yard releases the news that they have caught a suspect. No further details are provided due to the ongoing investigation. We are caught by surprise. We didn't see it coming.

No further details are provided. No further details are provided?

No further details can only mean this or that, something murky. No further details can only mean the Mainstream Media will speak of a Lone Wolf. No further details can only mean the Mainstream Media will not speak of a Lone Wolf. No further details can only mean the suspect is black, can only mean the suspect is white, can only mean the suspect is like this or like that, can only mean the suspect has a beard and a Middle Eastern name, that is has a name. No further details and the suspect will be insane or the suspect will not be insane and insanity will or will not be discussed. No further details and somehow a new shitstorm will ensue. Another shitstorm will be born. Another shitstorm in which we end up trapped for days. Another shitstorm in which we'll die in proportion to the worlds we excrete into the world. Another shitstorm and I can't even and I can't begin to and here I fixed your headline and thread and a lot of clapping between words in uppercase.

There's always a lot of clapping.

o o o

American TV; live.

A cam model accuses the President of the United States of America of sexual harassment. Stacy P — her professional name — says that she was groped by him during an event where she was a hostess. Allegedly he also flashed his penis at her, long enough for her to get her phone out and snap several pictures. This act of fixing the President of the United States of America's genitals for eternity could have been as much the result of a determination to sooner or later bring the events to the light, as it could have been a symptom of the zeitgeist and our need to capture every moment as images. Why did you take the pictures? I didn't really think that much to be fair — I just did it — I don't know why. The TV presenter remains unconvinced but every second counts on live television, so an extended silence is always unjustified. Did he just come to the toilet and expose himself to you? Just like that? Yes, he did, says Stacy P; he could have been drunk, she adds, although the President of the United States of America is supposedly a teetotal, as the presenter reminds the audience. I'm pretty sure he was drunk and I'm absolutely sure his breath smelled of alcohol, says Stacy P.

This is more or less the gist of what the American public finds out that night, in that ten minute interview.

The event where the presidential exposure allegedly took place was a fundraiser organised by a weapons manufacturer in support of the campaign that would see the President of the United States of America snatch a victory that surprised the whole world. The location of the event was one of the hotels that the President of the United States of America owns somewhere in Florida, generally a holiday destination for the old and dying but also a conference centre, one that since the start of his presidency serves the role of an unofficial parallel White House. The matter supposedly had been resolved privately, after the President of the United States of America agreed to pay an undisclosed sum for Stacy P's silence and the deletion of the pictures. And she kept quiet and deleted the pictures — or that's what she swears and so far the pictures haven't seen the light. It's unclear why she decided to come out with this story now but the gossip is judged newsworthy and perhaps it is. So suddenly most TV channels and online and print publications are banging on about it, giving her time and pages to discuss her ordeal, as well as to provide several details about the genitalia of the most powerful pervert on earth: I can describe his penis very well, she says, involuntarily quoting a moment in 80s classic *Porky's*, something that doesn't go missed by a couple of amateur film critics.

Many well-reputed political commentators — men and women — fall for the temptation to discuss the American President's dick, in a move that some argue is hypocritical, as it's been some time since it's been acceptable to engage in the once favoured sport of discussing a female politician's tits, legs, or bottom, and yet here we are talking about this elderly man's penis. Many male politicians, presenters, TV personalities, social media users, bring this up, betraying perhaps a certain unhappiness with their own genitalia, or the concern that a backlash against the presidential dick might end up involving them too — if you shake the tree long enough apples will fall, and the same might be said of shaking a dick. But perhaps they are right, and there shouldn't be space for bodyshaming anyone, regardless of their gender. Nevertheless, Stacey P's declaration that the President of the United States of America's genitals resemble three raisins left in water for too long deserves at least a modicum of attention due to its studied poetic spontaneity.

It's not the first time the President of the United States of America has been accused of sexual misbehaviour — the list is long and includes women from every walk of life, from politics to journalism to the service industry to retail to secretarial staff and even a former nun. Nothing new, but this is the first time the media really seize on the opportunity and go for him – his declining image rating might have something to do as much as the soundbites provided by Stacy P.

The supporters of the President of the United States of America suspect Stacy P might have been encouraged by their nemeses, for her to bring this to light at this moment. They also suspect the pictures exist somewhere and that the President of the United States of America's raisins will sooner or later end up flashing on millions of screens. Meanwhile, the opposition suspect that the President of the United States of America has staged this "scandal" (they actually use quotation marks to talk about it) in order to keep everyone focused on his genitalia and distracted from the accusations that he might have received money from a Middle Eastern oil company in order to loosen restrictions on fracking in national parks. A lesser damage to his image, they reason, as not many of his male sympathisers will care about this new act of misogyny, and some may even celebrate it. Not to mention the narcissistic pleasure of having the whole world talk about his penis, they add.

Many articles are written in the days that follow the

revelations, from those praising Stacy P for coming forward against a very powerful man, to those attacking the sexism of the arms industry, arguing for proper equality in the sector, to others attacking the cam model for the timing of her accusation and her loose morals.

But there's also space for marketing and soon the country's biggest raisin farmer — based in California and actually not that big — seizes the opportunity, releasing a promoted tweet with a picture of a fistful of their raisins lying on top of an American flag: SIZE DOES MATTER — AMERICAN RAISIN CO. It's a very successful commercial tactic and soon many financial commentators in the media are speaking of the audacity of American Raisin Co. Even the President of the United States of America celebrates their intelligent ploy, adding that it's always the case when his own raisins are involved in a certain situation that everyone comes out a winner.

But his comments don't stop his followers from boycotting American Raisin Co. The boycott in this case entails not buying a product they had never bought before. Meanwhile, liberals and leftists embrace American Raisin Co and celebrate their bravado. The Californian raisins — produced mostly by immigrant labourers in rather precarious employment conditions — become a symbol of their struggle against the President of United States of America. For a couple of days, at least.

o o o

The events take a dark turn a week later when Stacy P plunges to her death from the balcony of her seventeenth floor in Brooklyn.

She lands on top of a parked Ford Explorer and her naked body ends up broken and contorted on the car's roof. Much like the famous picture of a New York blonde, dead several decades ago, suicided and aesthetically sprawled over a car roof in golden ratio fashion after jumping from the Empire State building — a death that will live forever as an iconic photo. But in the case of our cam model no beautiful photo will prevail. There's no aesthetic death for her, just broken bones, a deformed skull, and her eyes filled with blood from the internal damage, as the pictures taken by passersby will show for those of us willing to see, generally many of us, on sites like Real Gore and Dead-Leaks, on WhatsApp groups, in the privacy of our rooms, during moments of relaxation.

No suicide note will be found; no witnesses to the moment of her death. No CCTV images captured her fall either, due to a technical malfunction that turned the whole building into a blind surveillance spot. Obviously the suicide soon gives way to constellations of speculation, from those of us blaming the CIA, to those speaking of Russian agents trying to smear the President of the United States of America even if Russia more or less fixed the election that crowned him, to those blaming the Illuminati, to those blaming the Rothschilds, to those accepting that it is indeed a suicide, but one motivated by some satanic disposition or something equally anti-Christian and un-American. Even stupider theories are entertained, but most fail to gain enough momentum to be noticed.

Some friends come forward to speak about Laurianne's — her real name — struggles with substance abuse and bipolar disorder. These friends reject the claims that her breakdown came after her experience with the President of the United States of America, or that she could have been killed — it was bound to happen, she was a disaster in the making for at least a decade. Other acquaintances — including a barista from her local coffee shop, a Latino of undisclosed origin who apparently was on very friendly terms with her — will come forward to declare she had been quite merry lately, something that the pundits on Fox News take as a sign of an impending suicide — people don't kill themselves when they are down, they do it when they are at the top, says one of their presenters. CNN take her recent happy mood as a clear indication of foul play. Speculation is rife. Never has the death of a cam model meant so much to so many.

A preliminary autopsy reveals no sign of physical violence save that of the impact. It also reveals high levels of cocaine in her blood. The NYPD coroner quickly comes forward to declare to the media that the case – although it must be left to run its course – is not currently being treated as suspicious. There are no signs to indicate that any foul play has taken place and there are no signs of violence or struggle in the deceased's domicile or on the body, while none of the many neighbours around, above and below her, saw or heard anything that raised their suspicions. The coroner attributes the traces of cocaine in her blood to the fact that the substance is popular in certain circles, we demand that The Public and The Media stop with their helpless conspiracy theories and let the authorities proceed with their investigation.

Her long estranged father comes forward some hours after the press conference, to speak of a murder. The former truck driver from Fairhope, Alabama, starts touring all the TV channels that are willing to give him air time in the days that follow his daughter's death, pushing this version of the events. Laurianne was murdered, he explains several times in his colourful southern English full of references to God and The Divine, because she had tried to commit suicide several times before, needless to say failing every time, but more importantly always leaving a suicide note – she wasn't the kind of girl who'd leave everyone guessing. He takes his hand to his heart and swears, on everything that's sacred, that he has nothing to gain from this, that he even voted for the President of the United States of America.

Soon this becomes the official version for half the country: she must have been killed to keep her quiet. The Deep State the President of the United States of America once denounced is acting on his behalf; the swamp he was supposed to dry is still sucking in innocent people. Even some of his most loyal followers start turning against the President of the United States of America, privately and publicly. Maybe it was only a matter of time. They've been betrayed, just like the trucker from Fairhope, Alabama. They haven't lost a child, yet, but that too can change. The word "traitor" starts making the rounds on Twitter, deployed around references to family values and the American Way of Life. The fact that Laurianne was white and blonde helps to fan the outrage and many are willing to forget about her profession. The Church of Westborough, on the other hand, scrambles their disciples and organises a demo in Brooklyn, across the road from the scene of Laurianne's tragic end — they demand all *camwhores* burn in hell. They demand The President of the United States of America burns in hell. They demand New Yorkers burn in hell. They demand everyone burns in hell. They demand to burn in hell as well.

And so it seems that The President of the United States of America will fall, that this could be the straw that broke the camel's back, even if there is no direct indication of his involvement, or the veracity of the now deceased cam model's accusation, even if she's believed on social media, with hashtags, and posts reminding everyone of her name. Until much to the bad luck of the estranged father who is touring the TV talk shows, North Korea resumes its nuclear weapons programme after an attempt at peace with the South just before summer went sour over a minor disagreement regarding the catering on the negotiation table in the buffer zone, with the President of the United States of America pulling out of the talks.

o o o

A missile is fired from Unggi, across the Sea of Japan. It flies over Sapporo and lands three hundred kilometres from the shore, in the North Pacific Ocean. The island's alarm system automatically alerts the people to run for cover and prepare for the worse. Those awake to see the alert delivered to their mobile phone panic, obviously, and rush to hide in cellars and under beds due to the lack of official bunkers, but it's still too early for a mass panic and the reality is that most of the people in Sapporo sleep through the whole thing. It's another false alarm and the missile might as well be carrying potatoes, for no explosion is registered in the area where it lands. But this doesn't stop the news channels from all over the world transmitting the missile crisis live, summoning panels of experts, professors from here and there (lots of beige as usual), and reminding the audiences about the gravity of the situation, the death toll of the Korean War of 1950-53, the potential number of casualties of an artillery attack on Seoul (The Corridor of Death, they call it), the possibility of deploying more American nuclear weapons in South Korea, or moving a large number of troops to be ready if an invasion is deemed necessary. This is a new Missile Crisis, many agree, capturing the zeitgeist, surrendering to the need to come up with facile and frequently inaccurate historical comparisons. Considering the recent tensions with Russia over who gets to bomb Syria, the world is living a new Cold War and sides are becoming clearly defined. Leaders must show restraint. Human existence is hanging by a hair, as always, but now it's different.

When the time difference allows for an intervention, The President of the United States of America takes to Twitter to threaten the tinpot dictator of the North with fire and a rage like the world has never seen before, not even in Hiroshima and Nagasaki. The tweet enrages many of us, due to the dubious taste of the comparison, considering the non-nuclear missile was fired over Japan, that Japan is an ally, and that most Japanese people regard the nuclear annihilation of a considerable amount of their citizens as something they'd much rather not see repeated, whether that be with North Korean or American bombs. Nevertheless the tweet is shared generously, and the message is delivered to the appropriate parties. The American political class starts aligning around or against the words of the President of the United States of America, and soon nothing else matters – there may be a war after all. And perhaps the world needs a war. A war always puts things in perspective. A war might be what we need, in order to put an end to our stupor.

Seizing on this demand for grand narratives, The Pope – still reeling from the latest scandal, in which one of the men of his inner circle was accused of fucking enough kids to fill St Peter's Square – intervenes. Tweeting from his different accounts, in several languages, he invites The President of the United States of America and the North Korean leader to enter dialogue – there is a common ground and that ground is our shared humanity, he says. The message is warmly received, particularly among the broadsheet-reading elite, who have taken to liking the Holy Man, maybe because he comes from the Third World and tends to engage in exercises of humility and is charismatic enough to smile for the camera. But elsewhere – particularly in the comment sections of the tabloids – the reception isn't very warm and the messages are frequently used to remind the Pope about the kiddy-fiddling scandal. A few Catholics (one would assume) get offended by these references and use the opportunity to remind everyone that they can that Muslims are also kid-fuckers when they make up their minds that they want to fuck kids, just like those grooming gangs a couple of years ago, the police cover up, political correctness gone mad, let's call a spade a spade, no one ever talks about this any more because pedophilia only matters when it's about white nonces. Some – one would suspect the aforementioned broadsheet readers, commenting in the wrong place as an exercise of expiation — make use of the occasion to remind everyone that the cases were very much in the news, being used as an excuse to do some Muslims-bashing, particularly by far right politicians who might also be kid fuckers but so far have managed to keep it quiet. Heated arguments start to take place between these rather loose two demographics. And then atheists join in, reminding the world that everyone who has ever been involved in any religion, in any form, is an idiot, and then post-secular leftists join in, praising the good aspects of religion, and some of the bad ones too, and insults are exchanged, and someone calls someone a luvvie, and someone else calls someone else a gammon or some other charcuterie term, and the message of peace gets diluted, while everyone debates whether processed meat is racist or not.

After his failed intervention, the Pope stays out of the argument and only tweets again a couple of days later, when he reminds the world about this or that aspect concerning greed or the environment.

o o o

In the days that follow the new North Korean missile launch many develop a sudden expertise regarding all things nuclear, ballistic, and strategic. The New Missile

Crisis is followed live on television, blogs on newspapers, Twitter moments, hashtags, comments on Facebook. The whole world is watching, waiting for the smallest thing to be announced. But instead of novelties we are fed repetition — the same opinion is remixed several times, turned into a cubist opinion: eaten, chewed, swallowed, excreted and eaten again. But we can't stop watching, reading, consuming, despairing about the state of the world.

Some chosen few remain hooked to the death of the cam model, even as the American fleet starts drilling in the Sea of Japan with their South Korean counterparts, a move that most experts read more as a dissuasion tactic than one with a clear military objective. They don't get fooled by what they judge are the President of the United States of America's attempts to direct public opinion towards another place (a tactic favoured by American presidents of all persuasions since the early days of the great nation of the North). Yet that doesn't stop them from also speculating as to what a war between the USA and North Korea would look like, whether China would feel compelled to join in, what the Russians would do, what the Japanese would do, the approximate death toll of such a conflict, the inevitable nuclear hecatomb that would follow, whether any life would remain on earth. The possible conflict needless to say is deeply fascinating. And it drips into everyday life, tainting everything with a tragic patina: everything everyone does could be the last thing someone ever does, anywhere in the world. The bunker industry makes huge gains, with garden bunkers becoming a best seller in Hawai and California. The sex industry also sees huge gains: YourPorn, the world's favourite procrastination portal, where all of the tragic cam model videos can be found for free but with ads sees its traffic multiply times ten, as the world turns to desperate masturbation in a very likely failed bid to ease the stress of a nuclear holocaust looming in the horizon. Why we choose to masturbate watching videos of a dead person is hard to say. Maybe it's just a coincidence; maybe it's a way of reaffirming life.

o o o

And then everything comes to an end but not The End, when North Korean leaders meet their South Korean counterparts, out of nowhere, unexpectedly, and talks about denuclearising the peninsula make the headlines once more. Yes, almost as if a déjà vu, a repeat of late May and many other times before, the North wants to denuclearise the peninsula, and they say it in the most unequivocal of terms, with an official communiqué that sounds very much like a John Lennon B side from the monstrous Imagine, and another trip to the border, and a lot of handshaking and smiling. In all fairness "unexpected" doesn't cut it. No one could have anticipated — again — this turn of events, not only two weeks after the tinpot dictator from the north *allegedly* fired a missile over Sapporo (the media start using the term allegedly; print media start using italics too). No one saw this one coming, certainly not The President of the United States of America, who declares first on Twitter and then to the Mainstream Media that caution needs to be taken, that action speaks louder than words, and no action has taken place so far, beyond the action of speaking [sic], and this is not the first time we see this, so caution must be had. Asked if he will take part in the negotiations he responds affirmatively, as long as he is required to take part. But as the days go by he isn't invited and soon it's clear that if peace is ever achieved between the North and the South it won't involve him — perhaps it will be achieved as long as it doesn't. The South Koreans diplomatically make sure to communicate this to the press, that they can manage by themselves, thank you, and that if the valuable input and support of The President of the United States of America is ever required this will be requested from him and the world in the expected way and via the official channels.

This snub is rightly portrayed as a snub both by chummy and antagonistic media. And soon the comments start coming in at 200mph. Some declare that the snub is an insult to the American People, while others write that anyone in their right frame of mind would want to keep The President of the United States of America as far from the negotiating table — and anywhere else — as possible. Others say that a peace that doesn't involve the United States of America as guarantor is only half a peace. And others declare exactly the opposite, and others prophecise that the way things are going the only thing we can be sure of is that in some months from now the truce will be broken and the tinpot dictator from the North will be firing missiles once again, and the world will soon come to end, after almost snatching a peace deal.

And then the North Koreans go quiet.

And then the South Koreans go quiet.

And then even the President of the United States of America goes quiet (at least about this topic).

The opinion pieces, live blogs, and news article about an impending nuclear conflict stop coming in. The opinion pieces, live blogs, and news articles about an impeding truce between the countries start coming in instead. And then they stop. And soon we direct our attention to other things.

A male celebrity with a history of domestic abuse publishes a racist novel that gets the hatchet job in a national newspaper and everyone is full of glee and agrees that the novel is really bad but for some reason – maybe because it was covered in the national press and widely discussed on social media – it becomes a bestseller. Another film producer is accused of sexual harassment and several Hollywood stars come forward to speak of the cases of abuse, and a film director who married his ex-wife's daughter gives an interview warning that many of those who came forward are careering on the bestselling topic of abuse, that sooner or later we'll get to the point where a man won't be able to speak to a woman, that we are heading towards a new Puritanical era. Around twenty new women come forward to accuse him of being a serial creep. And no one comes to his defence mainly because it's a known fact he is one. And then a white boy from Alabama is bullied by his black schoolmates, for the sole reason of being white and having a pronounced stutter. Keith, the name of the boy, doesn't want to go to school anymore – his life is made hell on a daily basis. He even recorded a video in his mother's car, in which he cries like the child he is, wondering why people are so evil, why someone would get pleasure from making his life hell. It's a heartbreaking video and it goes viral and Keith starts trending. Many celebrities take to his defence – bullying, everyone agrees, has no place in modern society. Football stars, baseball stars, basketball stars, Hollywood stars, Broadway Stars, the Karachians and their current sexual partners and even members of their entourage, everyone takes to Twitter, Instagram, Facebook, Snaptchat, Tumblr, Youtube, blogging platforms, any platform, to express their support for Keith – *#IStandByKeith* becomes a call to end school bullying once and for all and Keith becomes a national and international icon. His face – covered in tears and snot – appears on every screen. He's interviewed by Fox News, who frame his case as a case of reverse racism; this spawns a shitstorm of its own. Some argue that black people can't be racist to white people while others argue the opposite. Privilege checks and racist slurs are traded online until accounts are blocked, others voluntarily abandoned. The following week another video appears, once more featuring Keith. In this new video he's giving a nazi salute before a Confederate flag. This video was filmed by his mother as well; how it was leaked no one knows. A comedian known for his sharp tongue simply tweets *#KKKeith*. Some of us find his mocking of a kid with a stutter offensive; others find it hilarious. A lot of opinion pieces are written about Keith, bullying, racism, class, political correctness gone mad, political correctness not gone mad, the Karachians. And then, one morning, out of nowhere, after a couple of days of silence, the President of the United States of America says something racist about Mexicans and everyone starts talking about it and now it's mainly about debating whether all Mexicans are crooks and rapists or none of them are. And then the President of the United States of America says something about this or that journalist. And then he says something about Muslims. And then he says something about gays. And then he says something about blacks. And then something about women. And then the pictures of President of the United States of America's raisins start doing the rounds on Twitter. But the images are blurry. And no it isn't him and yes it is, it's definitely the raisins left for too long in water. But something else happens and then something else. And someone says something, someone always says something, and then someone else says something else, and like that it goes on. And it goes on. And on. And on.

And then the President of the United States of America gets re-elected for a second term.

o o o

Dr Turner's disappearance from the public eye continued, unbothered, unstoppable. It was only a matter of time, after all. until his name stopped meaning anything, until it was swallowed whole by inescapable oblivion. The death threats were forgotten. And the threatening stuffed teddies that had by some delusional design turned up at his house and surgery were soon forgotten too.

Forgotten also were the two teenagers from North Carolina who got arrested for stuffed toy terrorism, after committing the unbelievable stupidity of including a return address on one of the parcels they sent. Jonathan and Mariah Cruz their names – second generation American siblings of Puerto Rican heritage. Forgotten they were in time, yes, as were the schoolmates and teachers who in the days that followed their arrest stepped temporarily into the limelight to speak of the abject normality of the Cruzes: no one saw it coming, they were very polite, a bit taciturn and rather reclusive, and perhaps a bit on the side of not very clever if not outright stupid – just two unremarkable Latino teenagers, not even mass-murder material, very American, their house flew the flag, there were Iraq vets in the family; nothing, there was nothing that anyone could have suspected from them, they never asked strange questions, their father coached the baseball team, and so on. Even the focus on their origins, however far back in time the Puerto Rican connection had to be traced in order to find someone born out of the USA quickly receded into the background. Sadly all this oblivion didn't help their case in any way, as they were taken to court on suspicion of committing an act of terrorism and everybody knows the American justice system has a penchant towards incarcerating the black and the brown, by coincidence or design.

But their disappearance from the spotlight and into the dark and damp disciplinary environs of the state, in a matter of weeks, did certainly help the case of Dr Turner's journey from the centre of the shitstorm to the outskirts and sooner or later into calm. What happened to the Cruzes no one knows and if someone ever did no one would care. Maybe in some years someone will write an article about them, dig them out of a cell, if they are still inside and didn't hang themselves from a rod, shoot a documentary for Netflix, write a piece full of typos for a local newspaper. But it's dubious that someone will care to dig their story out: there was nothing interesting about their plight, and there are many more remarkable criminals to worry about.

After some months the police custody was deemed unnecessary — something Dr Turner agreed with and that he would have preferred had happened sooner. Soon he re-opened his clinic and perhaps because of this return to a routine his life quickly sank into a soporific sense of normality. Few of his patients mentioned anything about what happened, beyond passingly and obsequiously referring to his ordeal, perhaps asking about the wellbeing of his family, to then start mumbling incoherently as Dr Turner started doing his work in their wide open mouths, talking about the weather, baseball, or about any other non-committal topic, as all dentists do when they want to forget that they make a living staring into and fidgeting with people's mouths. Yes, an ordeal, he believed that. It was an ordeal indeed, all because of that fucking lion and that sore bitch who sent his photo to that fucking rag The Daily Mail, that bitter and revengeful whore, he should have known better than to send her that selfie, that's true, but life is learning. It had been an ordeal. Everything had conspired towards that.

But soon it became clear even to him that the ordeal would have little significance when considered as just one episode in his life — it would be left behind sooner or later — it would stop mattering.

And time passed. And the word ordeal was ditched by the dentist.

o o o

Several years later everything is a distant memory or not even that. Dr Walter Turner, former dentist who retains his title in credit cards and all official correspondence as a matter of prestige, is now a retiree, perhaps not as wealthy as during his active years but with the benefit of time, experience, a good reputation, and better aim. It's now fifteen years since the Cyril Affair, as he likes to call it when reminiscing his misadventures for friends or family, and ten years since he divorced his second wife in order to start a relationship with his dental assistant Tamara, back when she still had her natural breasts, but already a peroxide blonde, and who was really supportive throughout the whole thing, even if he had to stop paying her for several weeks until they managed to reopen the surgery. He put hunting on an impasse — one can never be too careful — but sooner or later he was back shooting beasts (but never again with bow and arrow). In the past ten years or so he's hunted pumas in Patagonia, Muskox in Greenland, Wolverines in Russia, Rusa Deer in Mauritius, Red Brocket Deer in Mexico, Beicete in Spain, Pyrenean Chamois in the south of France, among other game. And then one day he finds himself back in Zimbabwe, this time hunting giraffes north of Bulawayo, not that far from Hwange National Park. Maybe he had do it. Maybe he had to come back, exorcise the memories, however latent these were. Or perhaps it was just a matter of pride. Perhaps even an unconscious feeling that he needed to take something from this country, that the Cyril Affair was perhaps a stain in an otherwise spotless hunting trajectory. Or maybe it's all down to chance and the fact he never killed a giraffe before and he wanted to tick that one off the list. Who knows what goes through his mind?

So in Zimbabwe he is, one way or the other.

This time, perhaps because he's wiser or perhaps because he's older and more tired, he's hired a hunting pack that includes a stay in a comfortable camp – it's more of an AirBnB than a camp, but the word *camp* produces the right effect. The service of a professional hunter is also included, as is a 4x4 vehicle to take him around. And because the hunting takes place within the confines of Mr Mark Sharpe's ranch – Mr Sharpe being one of the most well reputed peddlers of safaris in Africa – he doesn't need to worry about stepping into any forbidden area or killing any protected beast, or even hiring assistants (lackeys, as they used to call them) to carry his stuff under the scorching Zimbabwean sun, a practice that since his last incursion into the jungle has come to be badly regarded. He doesn't even need to worry about gun or ammo permits, as everything is included in the pack — he'll get a Browning X-Bolt Pro and a hundred wig mag 300 rounds and a sidearm, more than he needs to take a giraffe. Things in the safari and hunting sectors have advanced a great deal since the days of his Cyril Affair.

Ranch Sharpe it's called, and soon the 4x4 that picked him up from Joshua Mqabuko Nkomo International Airport is stopping in front of the tall gates. The driver, a large and bald white South African middle-aged man, who hardly speaks a word in the hour or so it takes him to drive from the airport to the ranch, gets off the 4x4 and walks towards the two black armed guards standing by the gates. From inside the car Dr Turner can see them shaking hands, betraying a familiarity that for some reason he finds comforting. He even finds comfort in their matching shirts and shorts, the uniform that betrays the professionalism of the whole operation; and he finds comfort in the guards bumming a cigarette from the driver, who, smiling, surrenders a crushed pack with three or four still left inside. The driver speaks to the guards for a couple of minutes, their voices can't be heard from the inside, and then one of the armed guards walks towards the car and waves with a big grin in his face, moved more by curiosity than deference. Dr Turner waves back, the other guard waves in turn, and soon the big South African man gets back in the car, the gates open, and some minutes later they are stopping by the main house in the ranch, after driving down an unremarkable road surrounded by tall grass that has been left to grow in order to give the scene an almost wild aura, but that instead makes everything look a bit unkempt. Without much ceremony he's led to the main ranch. Someone will take care of the bags, the driver says as closing line.

The reception party, waiting in the veranda outside of the main entrance, is comprised of Mr Sharpe and four other white men, all dressed in beige (shirts and shorts), and who are introduced to Dr Turner as members of a club from Russia, who are hunting in Ranch Sharpe for the first time. Mr Sharpe introduces them one at a time and handshakes are exchanged with the dentist but he fails to retain any of the names, not that he will need to pronounce them for anything, really, but it's always nice to remember names, if only to figure out that you can. Big men, hard faces, thick wrists, flat noses

— stereotypically Russian. Each one of the men is violently tanned and two of them have visible strap marks in their left arms, where a watch would otherwise be, something that Dr Turner reads as a sign they've been in the wild — in the ranch — for a couple of weeks.

After drink arrangements, facilitated by a black woman with short hair and dressed all in white, barefoot, the men sit around a circular sofa with a faux-leather tiger pattern, in a large reception room surrounded by windows, from where a vast stretch of land can be seen disappearing into tree lines. Here Mr Sharpe launches into a detailed monologue narrating the variety of animals in the ranch and the possibility of picking the *trophies* beforehand or paying as you go, he says, and laughs; Dr Turner laughs as well but the Russians just grin, either because they've heard the same joke several times before or because their English isn't that good, while Mr Sharpe's South African accent is as thick as it comes. After describing the size of the ranch, the history (it belonged to his grandfather), the fauna and the flora of what he calls my privileged neck of the woods, and after narrating a life spent shooting beasts that nevertheless he admires, loves, Mr Sharpe goes on to ask Dr Turner about his hunting credentials. This is done in the most amicable of ways, more out of politeness that the need to establish hierarchies, as it's very clear that everyone is welcome to hunt in Mr Sharpe's privileged neck of the wood, as long as the can pay for their hobby. So here comes Dr Turner's turn to monologue and describe his life of hunting in every corner of the world. Mr Sharpe, obsequious, nods throughout the enumeration of distant and not so distant places. Obviously Dr Turner omits any reference to the Cyril Affair and Mr Sharpe — wise — omits asking about it. *Omits* because there's no way he would have missed the connection — Dr Turner's name must still mean something in Zimbabwe, in the way some obscure pop stars are big in Japan. Whether the Russians know about the Cyril Affair too or not Dr Turner can't guess; what is pretty clear now is that they speak very little English, for Dr Turner's reference to a failed bear hunting expedition in Kirov (which he pronounces *Kairov*) goes unnoticed. As do his attempts to reassure the Russian party that the failure of said expedition had nothing to do with Russia and everything to do with the fact that he suffered from food poisoning whilst in Finland, for which he decided to call the Russian adventure off. Mr Sharpe does laugh and then adds something about the expertise of Russian hunting guides, all former army men. But the Russians just smile in agreement, as they have been smiling for the past half an hour or so, regardless of what is being discussed.

Perhaps because he catches Dr Turner looking around, looking for something to make time go faster, Mr Sharpe invites his guests to visit the trophy room. This is at the back of the building, he informs them; the trophies are kept there, in a controlled environment – the Zimbabwean humidity would see to them otherwise. Mr Sharpe gets up and starts walking and so does the rest of the committee, the Russians following behind, carrying their drinks in their hands, with the ice rattling against the glass. Here Dr Turner realises Mr Sharpe has a pronounced limp, the kind you would expect to find in someone with a missing leg. This adds to the character, as would his personal history, if Dr Turner knew that Mr Sharpe is a former mercenary who lost his right leg after stepping on a landmine planted by Liberian guerrillas in the early 1990s. Of course Mr Sharpe doesn't go around telling this to the guests, unless he can be sure the information will be well-received. But these days he can't be sure anymore.

Soon they get to their destination.

The trophy room is exactly how one would expect a trophy room to be: animal heads and tusks and horns of all kinds, hanging from a wall that is covered on a red fabric that could very well be a carpet; skins on the floor (lion, zebra, some other unrecognisable beasts); bows and arrows and spears and shields, all melancholically tribal, one would think not direct results of hunting expeditions but there to add ambience – it's a stunning spectacle, to anyone interested in hunting. And as these men are interested in hunting indeed, there's some WOWs and whispers – they are clearly very impressed by the trophy room. Two of the Russian guests move towards one of the walls, to observe the tribal stuff; Dr Turner stays in the middle of the room, fixed on a beheaded lion staring back at him, whilst the other two Russians stay behind. Mr Sharpe looks at his guests in silence, grinning, managing his time well. And so there's something awkward about the situation, like too many men in silence in the same small room isn't something natural – and it certainly is awkward for these men, these hunters more used to vast expanses of tundra and animals charging at them than to the intimacy reduced spaces demand, the possibility of these shared moments of tension, or of their bodies accidentally touching another masculine body. Luckily, ever the crowd pleaser, Mr Sharpe clocks the silence has gone on for too long and soon launches into the history of some of the animals now hanging from the walls, recounting the places where he killed them and the guns he used, providing anecdotical details about each particular death, and introducing changes of pace and tone in his narration, that not only provide some colour to his words but that actually deem his very likely fabricated stories interesting if not fascinating. Out of habit, he performs his part with the proficiency of a lecturer delivering the same lecture for the 20th time, and the Russian guests seem mesmerised by his words, or the sound of his words, his body language, his aura, something. Fascinating, yes, but Dr Turner doesn't register anything at all, concerned as he is with the beheaded lion, and the two Russian men talking behind him, in Russian, obviously; they might be whispering but he's almost sure he's heard something that sounded like Cyril. Cyril and giggles. Or maybe it's his imagination and it's just a word that sounds similar to Cyril, some Russian word, like Cyrillic and giggles about this or that completely unrelated to anyone in this room. And he might be imagining their giggles as well, or they could be giggling about Mr Sharpe, or just laughing at one of his jokes (he seems to be making jokes too, which would mean they speak English after all), or perhaps they are drunk — that's what Russians do, don't they? He should stop paying attention to them — he's paranoid. Finally he manages to reconnect with Mr Sharpe's words, at the exact moment the latter starts explaining that the trophies are prepared on site by a team of experts, and that they are included in the holiday pack (he actually says *holiday* and *pack*), as are all the taxes imposed by the Zimbabwean government on wildlife exports. And so on, and so on.

At some point the talk ends, they go back to the main room, and from here Dr Turner is led to his camp by the same woman who had prepared the drinks, who walks before him all smiles but silent, until the moment she tells him that breakfast will be served in his veranda the following morning, and that in the same place the hunter will come to meet him for his outing. And then she walks away and Dr Turner watches her go, watches her bottom walk away because that's what a white man should do with a black bottom, until she disappears towards the left, behind some trees. And he's left alone in the camp.

So the camp.

The camp is actually a small room with fake grass roof and fake stone walls – it looks like the typical American affair, except there's no swimming pool visible and no other equally prefabricated rooms full of unemployed artists and prostitutes around. It's a motel room in the middle of nowhere. There are mosquito nets on the windows and door, which are open to let the late afternoon air through, even if the air is still hot and muggy. The room isn't that big but there is a double bed and the space is more than enough for one person, a large TV set, and a bar with all sorts of bottles. Crossing the other door there's a small toilet with a bath tub that takes half the space — the mirror is big without lacking masculinity, and hanging from a wall a large medicine kit that should contain all the essentials for survival during his adventure: from bismuth subsalicylate to snake antivenom and perhaps even condoms.

Back in the room. His suitcases are already waiting for him, as is the Browning X-Bolt Pro, laid on the bed next to a gun with ammunition and a cleaning kit, and a Smith & Wesson Highway Patrolman — a not so subtle .357 but efficient, not at all prone to jamming, a classic gun, faithful and likely to please the romantic, not that he can be much bothered as it's just a sidearm and he's never used any sidearm while hunting, except one time he had to nail the tent pegs. But the Browning — it's a beautiful piece of engineering, no doubt; he can't wait until he gives it a go tomorrow but there'll be time to shoot it during the week. There's also a pair of slippers, a bathrobe, and some personal hygiene items waiting on top of the night table — a toothbrush comes particularly handy, as he has forgotten his own back home, the irony. There must be a bible in the drawer but Dr Turner doesn't bother checking. Everything is very satisfactorily clean and attention has been paid to detail, perhaps too much, which shows the changing demographic of the sport, with hunting becoming a family hobby, particularly after the endorsement of the Former President of the United States of America, may he rest in peace. In any case he's come to hunt, not to waste time thinking about the decor.

Dr Turner sorts out his shirts and shorts in the wardrobes in the corner of his camp. After having a shower and going over the essentials such as connecting his phone to the wifi and texting the peroxide blonde (the second one) to announce that he has arrived safely and is ready to start his adventure the next day, he gets in the bed and prepares to have a good rest, and then a good sleep, after watching television for a while. The screen flashes a couple of times and then high frequency sounds fill the room and then the image bursts from the middle of the screen to the sides. He's expecting a Zimbabwean TV show, perhaps the news, a foreign and exotic television studio, a very likely white presenter dressed in colourful clothes, and incomprehensible talk about something he doesn't care about in the slightest. But instead he's welcomed by CNN and a black presenter dressed in dark colours. As expected they are covering the ongoing funeral of the Former President of the United States of America; they have covered barely anything else in the past weeks. Yes, it was a scandal when the tape of him giving the order to sort out the cam model and make it look like a suicide turned up. It was a disaster and the chaos unfolded at light-speed. And yes it was very good for ratings; the whole process of indictment and then a criminal trial, live on every American lounge, and seeing the Former President of the United States of America fall, lose his immunity as senator for the State of New York, be abandoned by his own people. And then, against all odds, he was declared innocent, the video was declared an AI-generated fake, and there were riots in several American cities, but then that was ages ago. And now it's the funeral and they are giving him the royal treatment, bouquets, escort cars, a 21-gun salute, and no mention of the *suicided* cam model. But to be fair today he's not interested at all in the story of the Former President of the United States of America, or anything to do with "back home" (he thinks on those terms, even if he's only away for two weeks). So zap zap, he changes channels — all in English, all covering the same shit in one way or the other, all about the Former President of the United States of America and his ridiculous hairdo and his fake tan and his narcissism and what he used to do, and what he used to say, and his slightly deformed children, and what his wife looked like, and whether she was happy or sad and a inextinguishable cesspool of stupidity. Zap zap, until he bumps into what looks like a Zimbabwean drama that could be a film or a soap opera, he can't tell. There's even black people in it and they are talking in their alien language, showing alien locations in unknown cities, driving in old cars over rutted dirt roads, old cars whose makes he can't recognise. They are these characters he can't relate to in any way, perhaps going over existential predicaments that make no sense to him, or to which he wouldn't be able to connect even if he understood, but that's the whole point, this disconnectedness – he never understood people who travel to reproduce their home abroad. Travelling is about immersing yourself in a foreign culture, even if you can't make sense of it, and even if you immerse yourself and all your previously conceived ideas remain unchallenged. It's about the immersion, really. Watching the local telly. Eating the local food even if you hate it. Drinking the local drink. Shooting the local animals. And this is exactly what he's doing right now. And immersing himself in that alien culture that he'll never be able to fully unpack, thinking thoughts that he manages to half-notice and that would make excellent proper thoughts for someone trying to sustain a dialogue with himself, like that he falls asleep.

o o o

He is hunting.

The gun is loaded. The wind blows in the right direction, and at the right speed, the conditions are ideal. And the giraffe is there, static exactly in the middle of the crosshair; its head exactly in the middle of the crosshair; its right eye exactly in the middle of the crosshair. The stupid beast is even staring at him with that same beastly eye, munching at a leaf from a tree, its tiny ears fluttering in the periphery of the crosshair, perhaps to shoo the flies away, or perhaps involuntarily, a symptom of its stupidity. Unsuspecting, munching, staring at him, in total oblivion about what's about to happen, the death that will be unleashed soon, the existential hierarchy that will be re-established, re-enacted, in just a couple of seconds. That is the tragedy of animals: they never know what hits them, be it a bullet or natural death; they go through life without having a clue, munching their beastly food until BAM, a bullet between eye and eye and everything's over — go munch leaves in giraffe heaven. No notion of life or death for them, just present, just enough awareness to identify danger when it comes for a predator equally bestial. But totally unaware of a death delivered by technology, engineering, a human death — that thing shining in the sun, that thing so attractive, so interesting, that's the glitter of death, you idiot beast.

So no remorse in putting this giraffe out of its misery. He might be doing it a favour; it might reincarnate into something better, superior, maybe into a human being. This might be the role of the hunter, perhaps, to help these stupid beasts fulfil their destiny, to help them move up in the evolutionary ladder one reincarnation at a time. Help them die, and hope that in the very last breath they'll understand at least their death. Yes, then they must know, for once they must understand what's going on. It's impossible they won't know, for their death is the only thing that gives any meaning to their pathetic lives.

He breathes, his eyes fixed on the giraffe's forehead, following the way the muscles move and the skin tenses and relaxes with every bite and swallow, how it extends its teeth to grab a new leaf, that will be the last leaf you ever munch, you piece of shit, and the process of biting and gulping and on and on, another leaf, and now the teeth tracing a horizontal movement more than a vertical one, a fact that makes the animal look even more stupid. He hates the beast and yet he wants to help the beast — it's hard to explain, there's a thin line between love and hate. But hard to explain or not, he realises then and there that there isn't anything in the world that he wants more right now than to blow a massive hole in its forehead; he wishes nothing more than to see a red cloud of blood squirting from behind its head, like red mist reaching out for the skies, and then its deformed and weak and unnecessarily long legs giving in, the body collapsing, already dead, yet with the muscles still in automatic pilot and twitching, the pieces of leaf still descending through the digestive organs, life becoming arrested little by little, civilisation triumphing over the barbarity of nature thanks to a Browning X-Bolt Pro and its wig mag 300 rounds, the animal finally collapsing and dying, docile and thankful.

The time is now – he's ready. He breathes in, breathes out, his mind one with the giraffe, and presses the trigger.

And nothing happens, he must have pressed too lightly, he should have fired one bullet before to properly figure out the trigger, and now the momentum is gone. It's like a rhythm, he has to enter into the rhythm. At least the love or the hatred is still here. He breathes in once more, and then breathes out, and presses the trigger again and nothing happens, for the second time. This time he's sure he pressed the trigger all the way down. And he's sure he heard a muted CLICK. So he stops aiming at the giraffe, his temples beating with blood, and jerks the rifle to the left, loads the bolt mechanism, ejects the round in the chamber and checks it out: the base is marked – it's been shot. But he must be losing his head; he could have sworn he checked the three bullets in the magazine and that all were live; he remembers thinking two of those bullets were unnecessary, that he only needed one; he must be tired. Or maybe the bullet was empty. Maybe it's a faulty one. It could happen. It never happened to him before. But then who knows who casts the bullets for Mr Sharpe, because these are totally homemade bullets.

He gets the magazine out and checks the remaining rounds – the right weight, no sign of having been fired, and still one bullet too many, for only one will suffice to send the beast to Giraffe Hades, he'd never miss a shot like this, not in one million years. He loads another round into the chamber and aims his rifle at the giraffe again, checking his breathing, in and out, regaining the momentum, only that now the giraffe is Cyril the lion and the Browning Bolt X-Bolt Pro is a bow and he lets go of the arrow and it crosses the air towards Cyril almost as if in slow motion, like on Zeno's paradox, taking forever to reach its target, while he sweats, can feel the sweat dripping from his forehead and into his eyes, stinging his eyes, the sweat running down his back, and the arrow keeps going, until the lion — by chance? — turns around and starts running away from the arrow, and the arrow penetrates its right flank, and it's all the same, all the madness, all the humiliation, all happening again, even the teddy bears and the journalists, another failed marriage, and thank god the kids are now living somewhere else, fucking hell another shitstorm.

He wakes up covered in sweat and it takes him a few moments to realise he's not hunting but that he's about to hunt, that he's back in Zimbabwe.

What a stupid dream. What a terrible dream! So much venom, so much hatred. He's nothing like that. He doesn't hate a single living thing. That's not what hunting is about! Where the fuck did those ideas come from? Shooting to the head? What's the fucking point! Is he going mad? Is he getting Alzheimer's? And of course the bullets will be fine. He gets up from the bed, stumbles towards the gun, towards the bullets. There's a whole box of them and even the box looks professional enough — sturdy cardboard, dark cream in colour — even if it doesn't say where the bullets are manufactured. He removes some of them — they are all unfired and beautiful. Of course they would be. What a nonsense.

o o o

He couldn't see her face when she was standing outside, visible through the mosquito netting, but he's ninety percent sure it was the same woman, the one who had led him here yesterday, who knocked at his door to inform him the breakfast was served and waiting for him in the veranda. But it could have been some other black woman, because to him they all look the same, to be fair, not that he's racist or anything, but it's hard for him to tell one black person from another.

Breakfast. Veranda.

That was what he understood, half asleep as he still was. He wasn't really hungry but even then he had the presence of mind to remind himself he had to eat something, make sure to approach the hunting well-fed and well-hydrated, as it should be done, because it's physically demanding, and it'll be too hot. This chain of thoughts somehow told him that he was already focused. And this made him feel good about himself – he was in the zone already; in spite of that silly dream.

Yes, the dream. Just thinking about it and the dread comes back. Yes, the dream sucks. And yes, it's an unpleasant memory and he shoos it away telling himself that his mind is trying to play with him, that is easy to understand, being in Zimbabwe and not far from Hwange National Park, and the incident yesterday with the Russians, whether it was his imagination or not. It was in the air, how could he not dream about it? Everyone is entitled to their insecurities. And it isn't the first bad dream he has had, is it? So he gets over it finally and then stays a bit longer in bed, trying to summon merry thoughts, trying to visualise a good shot, the work of art that is a good clean shot, a humane kill, and thinking of this peroxide blonde he saw waiting for the flight in Diass, her immaculate dress sense, beautiful toes – no cheap nail varnish – poking out of her coral high heels, tight skin, young, untainted by motherhood, still not embittered by life, what a woman, and when he's ready and fully awake jumps into his slippers and rushes to the bathroom, to quickly empty his bowels and then have a shower, using the opportunity to fail to masturbate, in order to have a properly clear mind. It's what any hunter in his place would do.

In a matter of fifteen minutes since that black woman – or another black woman who looked similar – knocked at the door and he was stolen from his sleep he's sitting in the veranda, lifting a shiny silver cover, finding a large plate with brown toasted bread, some fruits impossible to recognise, others less exotic like tangerines and a banana, butter in a state of disintegration, yogurt and muesli. There's a large bottle of mineral water, dripping condensation on the table cloth, and a small thermos next to the plate and a small glass with milk, covered with a napkin — real like the tablecloth, not paper — in order to keep the flies and other assorted local insects away. In the thermos there's coffee, and it's not bad at all, perhaps a bit on the weak and sweet side, but coffee nevertheless, and it smells great, it smells like he was hoping African coffee would smell, even if this particular coffee is Colombian, not that he will ever find out. He finishes the first cup and while he's in the process of serving the second one, telling himself that the idea that coffee is not good for hydration is bullshit, he spots the 4x4 approaching the camp from behind the trees. He starts smiling before the 4x4 stops a few metres away, which it does presumably in order to keep the dust away from the camp. And by the time the arrival slams the door behind himself after getting off the car, his face is already hurting but his immaculate teeth are still protruding, incandescent. He watches the man — dressed in kaki shorts, a matching shirt, desert boots and a desert hat — walk towards him, still trying to hold the smile. And then he watches the man remove his hat, shake it a couple of times out of habit or for effect, and then hold it in his hands, and then close to his head, on a salute that looks as rehearsed as authentically friendly. It's the hunter, needless to say; everything about the man exudes hunting; he was born to hunt; there's nothing about him that doesn't say HUNTER, loud, very loud.

Soon they are sitting on the veranda, drinking from the same weak coffee, sharing hunting anecdotes, the hunter in order to show off his CV, Dr Turner in order not to lose the pissing contest without a fight. He's a nice man, Mr Thompson, the hunter. Another white South African with a fantastic accent and a toned body – an action man, revolver hanging from a holster on his belt and all. Very friendly. Funny – he makes some kind of joke that Dr Turner celebrates with laughter although he misses it, something of local overtones that the hunter shouldn't have said, but that perhaps he couldn't keep to himself, or perhaps that he didn't clock as cryptic to an American tourist. A cool man, no sign of rushing, no sign of anxiety, Mr Thompson – he gives Dr Turner his full attention. Hunting is a form of meditation after all – every trophy brings a hunter closer to perfection, to calm, to an absolutely calm mind. Maybe that's why we hunt. It has to be that, or something like that.

They talk some more, mostly about guns and the local animals. The conversation soon slows down, it starts to get repetitive. And this is taken as the sign that they must leave. Right, says the hunter, we need to get going. And soon they are in the 4x4, driving to pick up the Russians, who Mr Thompson informed will be shooting with them today, and the helper who will drive the pickup truck plus trailer, where they'll bring back whatever they take. Nice people, the Russians, Mr Thompson says, and he starts laughing and Dr Turner starts laughing too, accepting the invitation to be an accomplice in a bit of national stereotyping.

They laugh for a few moments and soon they are parking near the Russian camp, where they stop the car and the laughter and get off.

o o o

It's a pretty straight forward affair — it's impossible to miss a giraffe, really, and he'll be hunting with a proper gun, not a toy one, brand new, not a single scratch, exquisite sight, perfectly tuned, very light, colour blends with the background, none of that shiny and heavy old stuff, he should buy one of these X Bolts when he gets back home.

So the hunter drives the group to a corner of the ranch, and after a brief health and safety talk and an even shorter briefing RE the giraffes in the ranch and the likely places to spot them at this time of the day, the need to keep a safe distance in the unlikely event the giraffes decide to charge and kill you like that poor bastard in South Africa a couple of weeks ago, takes off with the Russians to track a lion further south, by the river that cuts the ranch in two, where the beasts are frequently seen when the sun starts burning. It's already 9:30am and it'll start burning soon and the lions will be out in the water before they go hide in the shade in the bushes. And there's a better chance to be eaten alive by lions than by a giraffe, so the hunter is more needed there than with the dentist. Plus they are Russians, and god knows what they might end up doing if left alone with guns, the hunter tells Dr Turner when the Russians are safely far away and both laugh. And like this, in high spirits, they split.

They've arranged to meet back by the road at midday, by the Pickup truck, to drive back to the main house, as it'll be too hot to hunt — they will reconvene after 6pm. The helper stayed in the Pickup. He insisted a couple of times in escorting Dr Turner during the hunt but the heroic dentist declined the offer, not without thanking him profusely, claiming he hunts better on his own. The truth isn't that far: he would have felt under pressure to perform if he'd had someone accompany him. He could have worded it differently, perhaps: he performs worst when not alone. Plus he has a radio, they all have them. His is off but he could turn it back on if he needed to. It's impossible to shoot straight with someone speaking on the radio, right?

So now Dr Turner is on his own, walking across the African savannah, carrying his Browning X-Bolt Pro behind his right shoulder, the Smith and Wesson safely stashed in its holster, binocular hanging from his neck, the thought of a giraffe nailed in his brain, becoming a part of its cortex. Our dentist in the wild, tracing the same steps as many before, feeling once more like the character in one of the novels he used to love as a kid, one of those hyper-masculine men with no *issues* whatsoever of any kind — ruthless hunters, killers, no different from a lion, pure energy, strength, aura — rulers of the world, who could very likely still get it up in the shower for a bit of solo fun.

o o o

It's incredibly hot and humid. There's a light breeze but more than a breeze it's the idea of a breeze, a formal breeze, just for the scenery, that amounts to nothing, a tiny detail. The leaves barely move on the trees; the air is nowhere to be felt, a non-air. It's like walking in a vacuum-sealed jar that's been left in the sun. A giant vacuum-sealed jar that contains the whole of Africa, and has been left under the African sun, if that makes any sense. Or like walking in a sauna, with a gun and with clothes on. He loves it.

East, 73 degrees more or less, according to the compass, not an iPhone, even if it works better; a proper compass, military, reference window with cross-hair, adjustable eye-piece, measuring slopes, none of which he's ever used. One foot after the other. Slowly, preserving his stamina for the precise moment – that moment of truth for which he's been preparing for days, or hours, or since he was born, or for which he was born ready, who knows. It feels like his head is melting under the hat. He's covered in sweat, there isn't any part of his body that isn't sweating, and his armpits are already stinking because he didn't wear deodorant, should his scent alert the prey. This is the hunter's way, this series of small sacrifices to which one surrenders voluntarily, perhaps just to prove to oneself that should the need arise – and it won't – one would able to deliver food to the table.

Just a few minutes ago he bumped into a small mound of tennis-ball sized turds in a clearing, next to a small pond the size of a double bed. Round, dark green animal droppings: giraffe's. Twenty or thirty little balls. He didn't count them but his experience told him it was twenty or thirty of them. He kneeled down and tested the consistency of one of the balls with a twig. It easily gave in, gifting to him its wet and dark green interior and the stench that only fresh animal feces can manage, that rather welcoming smell of crap that can't be told from the smell of wet grass: vegetarian shit. The distribution of the balls, the way they rested concentrated in an area of around half a square metre, with some pieces scattered in the same direction – betraying something done on the move – told him which way to go. The feces pointed east. A scrapped turd just a few metres down, crushed but not entirely flat, the giraffe's paw clearly visible on it, confirmed this initial reading. East it would be, more or less 73 degrees. And east he went.

So now he's walking in this open area with scattered trees, checking the compass every couple of minutes, scanning the horizon. The ground remains hidden below the tall yellow grass, but it's soft and he has to be careful not to stick his feet in a hole. Every time he moves a foot there is a swooshing sound – it's rather hypnotic. He moves slowly but secure, swoosh-swooshing his way across the Zimbabwean savannah, his rifle already pointing forward, hanging from its strap but already chambered, his side arm at the ready, the holster unclipped, feeling the long grass caress the front of his calves, occasionally reaching as high as his elbows. Swoosh-swoosh, swoosh-swoosh, and the occasional sound of a broken twig, the sole crushing a piece of dried mud, rolling over a rock. The eyes scanning for a head towering above the foliage, a tree that moves in a strange way, a figure crossing the landscape from left to right, or right to left – a giraffe – a target, something to kill. He can already anticipate having to dive to the ground, trying not to make a noise, using the long grass to camouflage, because no giraffe can be as stupid as the one in his dream, and there's no way it won't run away if it spots him. And he doesn't want to shoot it while running, no. This time he needs a good and clean shot – a shot to the heart, BAM, dead, even if a shot to the neck would have its beauty, the blood pouring from the two holes left by the bullet, the giraffe collapsing bent in two in the precise place where the shot entered and left the body. But not this time. Maybe another time, another giraffe, maybe even in this trip, while he's here, but this time a shot to the heart and a picture and then a bit of boasting with the rest of the hunting party, them and their stupid stinky lions, but never a selfie, never again. Just one good shot, a revenge of sorts, it'll be beautiful and the swoosh-swoosh of the grass and the cracking sound of a broken twig and something moves in one of the trees to the right and the movement that startles him and it could be a lion and he turns around but can't see anything and his heart beats faster, too fast, it bangs against the ribs, that intense pain in his chest and like this he falls to the ground, unable to put his hands forward.

He falls face first, still holding the compass, his eyes open, seeing nothing but grass, grass all around. He's stunned and has been taken by surprise but he's not too surprised to figure out what's going on. That's it. That's it. Just as those words cross his mind he feels his sphincters relax, piss and shit leaving his body, warm, messing his arse and his legs. It feels like it'll never end, the pissing and shitting. He doesn't want it to end. He would like to piss and shit himself forever, stretch this moment for an eternity, but that won't happen, of course it won't. And no life – no film of his best moments – crosses his mind, none of that nonsense, no memories of his wives, his children, his childhood, his first love, his trophies, the woman at the airport. Nothing crosses his mind but the thought that he's dying and the thought that he's pissing and shitting himself.

And here he understands.